July 6, 1989
love,
Carla

DEAR DIEGO

dear diego

ELENA PONIATOWSKA

Translated from the Spanish
by Katherine Silver

PANTHEON BOOKS, NEW YORK

Library of Congress
Cataloging-in-Publication Data
Poniatowska, Elena.
Dear Diego.
Translation of: Querido Diego, te abraza Quiela.
1. Rivera, Diego, 1886–1957—Fiction.   I. Title.
PQ7297.P63Q4713   863   85-45945
ISBN 0-394-55383-7

to jan

1947–1968

DEAR DIEGO

OCTOBER 19 · 1921

In the studio, everything has remained the same, my dear Diego, your brushes are in the glass and clean just as you like them to be. I treasure even the tiniest scrap of paper on which you have drawn a line. I sit down in the mornings to prepare the illustrations for *Floréal* just as if you were here. I have given up the geometric forms and now find myself drawing landscapes that are a bit painful and grey, blurry and solitary. I feel as if I could easily blur myself out of existence. I will send you a copy when it is published. I see your friends, especially Élie Faure, who is hurt by your silence. He misses you, says that Paris is empty without you. And if he says that, you can imagine what I could say. My Spanish is improving by leaps and bounds, and to prove it to you I am sending this photo on which I have written especially for you: "Your Quiela sends you many kisses with this picture, my dear Diego. Accept this photo until we see each other again. It didn't turn out very well, but with this one and the one I sent before, you will have something of me at least. Be strong as you have always been and forgive your Quiela's weakness."

I kiss you again,

Quiela

$\mathcal{N}$ OVEMBER 7 · 1921

Not one word from you and the cold is un-
relenting in its attempt to freeze us all to
death. A harsh winter is beginning and I
remember another one you and I would
rather forget. You even put down your
brushes to fetch fuel for the fire! Do you
remember how the Severinis carried a hand-
cart from Montparnasse all the way into
Montrouge, where they managed to get half
a sack of coal? This morning, as I put fuel
on the fire, I thought of our son. I remember
those wealthy homes with their luxurious
central heating—I think they had boilers
that ran on gas—and how the Zetings, Mi-
guel and Maria, took our child to their apartment in Neuilly to save his life. I didn't
want to leave you. I was sure that without

me you wouldn't stop working even to eat. I went to see the child every afternoon while you buried yourself in *El matemático*. I walked through the streets covered with black snow, all muddied with people's footsteps, and my heart was beating loudly because I knew I was going to see my little boy. The Zetings told me they would take him to Biarritz as soon as he recuperated. I was so touched by the care they took in looking after him, especially Maria. She would take him out of the crib—a beautiful crib like nothing little Diego ever had—with a nurse's care and tenderness. I can still see her pulling apart the white blankets and the embroidered sheet so I could get a better look at him. "He had a good night," she whispered happily. She would sit up with him at night. It seemed like she was the mother and I the visitor. That was, in fact, how it was, but it didn't make me jealous, quite the contrary, I thanked heaven for the Zetings' friendship, for young Maria's sweet hands fondling my baby. On the way home I would see the somber faces of the men on the street, the women wrapped in their mufflers, but not even one child. There was always bad news and the concierge made it her business to keep me up to date: "There is no milk in all of Paris" or "They say that they will have to shut down the municipal sewage system because there isn't enough coal to keep the machinery running," or even worse, "The water is freezing in the pipes and they are going to explode." "My God, we shall all perish!" A few days later, the doctor said that little Diego was out of danger, that the pneumonia was gone. Soon we would be able to bring him to the studio and get some coal, and the Zetings would come visit him and bring us tea, some of the tea they brought from Moscow. Later,

::

when you had less work, we would go to
Biarritz, the three of us together, the child,
you, and I. I imagined little Diego sun-
bathing, little Diego on your lap, little Diego
by the seaside. I imagined good and happy
days, as good as the Zetings themselves and
their house set in among those big pine trees
that make the air so clean and pure, as Maria
told me, a home where there were no priva-
tions, no rationing, where our child would
begin to walk, strengthened by the sun and
the iodine from the sea. When Maria Zeting
gave little Diego to me two weeks later, I
saw a flash of fear in her eyes, she covered
his little face with the edge of the blanket,
then hastily put him into my arms. "I would
have kept him with me for a few more days,
such a good little boy, so lovely, but I can
imagine how much you must miss him."
You put your brushes down when you saw
us enter and helped me settle the little
bundle into his bed.

══

I love you, Diego, right now I have an almost unbearable pain in my chest. In the street, there are moments when I am suddenly struck by your memory and then I can't walk and I feel so afflicted that I have to lean against a wall. The other day a policeman came up to me: "Madame, vous êtes malade?" I shook my head and was about to answer that it was love, you see I am Russian, I am sentimental and I am a woman, but then I realized that my accent would give me away and French functionaries don't like foreigners. I kept going, every day I keep going, I get out of bed and think that every step I take brings me closer to you and that the months you need to get settled—oh, how many!—will pass quickly and soon you will send for me so I can be by your side.

I cover you with kisses, your

Quiela

Today as never before I miss you and want you, Diego, your enormous presence fills the entire studio. I haven't wanted to take your jacket off the hook in the entryway, it still retains the shape of your arms, of one of your sides. I have not been able to fold it up or dust it off for fear that it would never regain its original shape and I would end up with a shabby old rag on my hands. Then I really would sit down and cry. That ragged old cloth keeps me company—I speak to it. How many mornings have I returned to the studio and shouted, "Diego, Diego!" just as I used to, simply because from the stairway I can see that jacket hanging near the door and I think you are seated in front of the stove or are looking with curiosity out the window. Nighttime is when I fall apart. In the mornings I can make believe and even face the friends I meet in the atelier. They ask what is going on with you and I don't dare tell them I haven't heard from you. I answer evasively, that you are well, working—it really embarrasses me that I can't tell them anything. Jacobsen wants to go to Mexico and he has sent you three telegrams care of the National University with paid replies and not one of them has been answered. Élie Faure was a bit ill and is upset by your silence. Everyone asks about you—well, at least at first, but now less and less—and it is so painful to me, my dear Diego, their silence combined with yours, accomplices in this terrible silence, even more glaring because our topics of conversation have always been you or painting or Mexico. We try to talk about other things, I see that they are trying, but soon they take their leave and I descend once more into my realm of silence that is you, you and silence, me inside silence, me inside you who are silence. I walk through the streets engulfed in your silence. The other day I saw Maria Zeting and I am sure she saw me, but she lowered her eyes and walked over to the other side of the street so as not to have to say hello. Maybe it is because of little Diego, maybe she feels sorry for me, or maybe she was simply in a hurry and I have become overly sensitive. I think now that you are not here, our friends are waiting to see what will happen. They relate to me *entre temps* until your return and in the meantime they do not visit me except to hear news about you. I accept the fact that they do not see me for me—after all, without you I am insignificant, my worth is determined by your love for me and I exist for others only to the degree that you love me. If you stop loving me, they could not love me nor could I love myself.

Once I had little Diego. It wasn't that cold any more in the studio—do you remember?—but every day we had to fetch coal. Even you went on one occasion, leaving your work right in the middle. I sensed that little Diego had not fully recovered. I could always hear a slight wheezing instead of that steady and silent breathing I had heard during his first days. I would go up to the crib at every anxious moment and this irritated you: "Nothing is wrong with him, Angelina, leave him alone, you are blocking his air." Our poor son! One night he began to moan terribly—and we knew there was a meningitis epidemic in Paris.

From then on he declined rapidly. The child whose little head had been lost among the sheets turned into one big head and you were horrified by this skull that was swollen like a balloon about to burst. You couldn't bear the sight, you didn't want to see it. The child cried incessantly. I can still hear those screams that grated so on your nerves. Whenever I hear a child crying in the street, I stop, I listen for that peculiar sound of little Diego's cries. The Zetings were no longer in Paris. I think you went out to fetch coal, you felt so impotent in the face of all that suffering. I remember one afternoon you tried to read the newspaper and your desperate gesture remains etched in my memory: "I can't, Quiela, I don't understand about anything that goes on in this room." You stopped painting. Little Diego died and we went alone to the cemetery. Marie Blanchard shed many tears, she always said that little Diego was her godson, the son she would never have. It was terribly cold that day, or maybe the coldness was inside me. You were absent, not even once did you speak to me, you didn't even budge when I took your arm. I gave the crib to the concierge, I gave her all of little Diego's things.

I thought that if I gave it all to her I would be able to ask for it back if we had another child. I always wanted to have another one, but you refused. I know that my life would now be difficult but at least it would have some meaning. It is very painful to me that you denied me a child. Having it would have made my situation worse, but my God! how much meaning it would have given my life!

I look at the grey sky and imagine your barbarously blue sky, the one you described to me. I hope one day to be able to contemplate it and in the meantime I send you all the blue I am capable of. I kiss you and am always yours,

Quiela

Yesterday I spent the morning at the Louvre, Chatito (I love calling you Chatito, it makes me think of your parents and I feel like part of the family), and I am dazzled. When I used to go with you, Diego, I listened to you with admiration, I shared your fervor because everything from you inspires me with such enthusiasm, but yesterday it was different. I *felt*, Diego, and it made me so happy. When I left the Louvre I went to the Vollard Gallery to see the Cézannes, and I stayed there contemplating them for three hours. Monsieur Vollard said to me, "Je vous laisse seule" and I thanked him. I cried as I looked at the pictures, I cried because I was alone, I cried for you and for me, but it was a relief to cry because it is spellbinding to finally understand, and I was treating myself to one of my greatest pleasures in life.

When I got home I began to paint passionately, and today I woke up feverish. I sat down in front of your easel and removed the canvas you left half done—sorry, Chatito, I will put it back soon—and I took out a clean canvas and began. It is impossible to be devoid of talent when you have the kind of revelations I had yesterday. I eagerly painted the head of a woman I saw in the street when I was returning from the Louvre, a woman with splendid eyes, and now that the light is gone I am writing to you about the commotion and my happiness. For the first time in four long years I feel that you are not far away, I am so full of you—that is, of painting. I plan to return to the Louvre in the next few days. I will go see another room, the one with the Flemish paintings you were so drawn to, and I will look at them with you, I will hold you by the hand, and I will also go back to the gallery with the Cézannes. The owner was very friendly and kind to me and this made my heart soar, I feel as if I have been reborn, so many years of devoting myself to painting, so many academies, so many hours in the studio, so much coming and going with you, and only yesterday the revelation. I write to you still trembling with emotion, my darling Chatito, and I hope that as you hold this white piece of paper you will be able to perceive that it is quivering between your fingers and you will be able to see me shaking and thankful and always yours,

Quiela

$\mathscr{D}$ECEMBER 17 · 1921

I haven't written to you for fifteen days because I have been sick, Diego. After my visit to the Louvre, I began to mark up a canvas in the heat of the greatest exaltation, agitated and with a headache. After a while I left the canvas and grabbed a pencil and threw out sketch after sketch, and when all the paper was gone, I picked up the sheets I had thrown away so I could draw on the other side. Nothing satisfied me. I woke up at four o'clock in the morning as you used to do and I tried to organize the composition. I kept at it all day, I struggled like you can't imagine, I didn't even get up to make myself something to eat. I remembered our stews made out of bones and a few vegetables—gruel, you used to call it—and I smiled to myself, thinking if only there was an Angelina who would take care of me and beg me to stop just for a minute to eat something. I continued throughout the night, convulsively, starting and stopping again and again. I thought that I had been possessed by your spirit, that it was you instead of me who were inside me, that this feverish desire to paint came from you and I didn't want to lose a second of being possessed by you. I even grew fat, Diego, I was overflowing, I couldn't fit into the studio, I was as tall as you. I battled with the spirits—you once told me you were in contact with the devil—and I remembered it at that moment because my chest expanded and my breasts, my cheeks, even my chin swelled, I was blown up like a tire. I looked in the mirror and there I was, with my swollen face throbbing as if it has been pumped up with a bellows. How my temples pounded! And my eyes! How red they were! It wasn't till

::

then that I felt my forehead and realized I had a fever. Blessed fever! I had to take advantage of it, live that moment in its totality. I felt you on top of me, Diego, they were your hands, not mine, that were moving. I don't know what happened afterwards. I must have lost consciousness because when I awoke in the morning I was cold and stretched out in front of the easel. The window was open. Surely I had opened it during the night, as you used to do when you felt as if your body was growing until it covered the walls, the corners, extending itself over a greater and greater expanse, going beyond its own borders. Naturally I caught a severe chest cold, and if it wasn't for the concierge's kindness, her daily *bouillons de poule*, you would right now be saying good-bye to your Quiela. I am much weaker, I haven't gone out, and except for Zadkin, who came over one afternoon to ask about you, my contact with the world has

been nil. My greatest happiness would be
to see a letter with a stamp on it from
Mexico among my scant correspondence,
but this would be a miracle and you don't
believe in miracles. I have been very ex-
cited; painting has been the central theme
of my meditations. I have been painting for
many years; I amazed the professors at the
Royal Academy of Fine Arts in Saint Petersburg, they said that I was much better than
the *moyenne*, that I should continue my
studies in Paris, and I myself believed in my
extraordinary aptitude. I used to think: I
am still a stranger in the land of painting,
but one day I will be able to take up resi-
dency. When I won the scholarship to the
Royal Academy in Saint Petersburg, oh
Diego! then I thought I really possessed
something wonderful, something I had to
protect and cherish at all costs. Paris would
be my final goal: l'Académie des Beaux-
Arts. Now I know that something else is

needed. Realizing this has wounded me so much, Diego, I can't even think about it without deepening the pain. Of course, I am promising, promising, but for how long have I been promising? I am still a promise. Sometimes your own suffering at the moment of creation consoles me and I think, If it was hard for him, how much more painful for me! But this thought does not comfort me for long because I know that you are already a great painter and you will become an extraordinary one, and I am painfully aware of the fact that I will not advance much beyond what I am now. I would need so much freedom of spirit, so much tranquillity in order to begin my masterpiece, and I am paralyzed by your memory besides all the problems you know by heart and I won't enumerate so as not to bore you: our poverty, the cold, the solitude. You could tell me how you have done it before, how anyone would envy my soli-

tude, that I have all the time in the world
to plan and execute a great work. But these
days I have been tossing and turning in my
bed tortured by the memory of our child
(and not engulfed like you by the flames of
the sacred fire). I know that you no longer
think about little Diego, you appropriately
cut yourself off, the branch once again turns
green, yours has become another world
while my world is that of my son. I search
for him, Diego, I miss him physically. If he
were alive, if he shared this studio with me,
I would have to get up no matter how bad I
felt and care for him, feed him, change him,
and just the fact that someone needed me
would give me some relief. But he is dead
and nobody needs me. You have forgotten
me there in that Mexico of yours that I
wanted so much to visit—the Atlantic separates us. Here the sky is grey and there in
your country it is always blue, and I strug-

gle alone without even the comfort of having sketched a few lines that are worthwhile
in the past few days.

Saying good-bye to you and kissing you
sadly,

Your Quiela

$\mathcal{D}$ECEMBER 23 · 1921

Floréal called for me again—they want more engravings. A *pneumatique* came and you have no idea how much joy that little piece of twice-folded paper gave me. The next day I went to Rue de Rennes, it was my first time out of the house. When Monsieur Vincent saw my deathly pallor he said, "Voilà ce que c'est l'amour." He wants ten illustrations, he and the editorial board loved the ones we did together before you left. I laughed to myself when I remembered how we painted the Russian emblem commissioned to me by the Czar's consulate in Barcelona and how well they paid us for the work we did on copper sheeting. The sea air came in through the window and you felt good, we painted in between the laughter, they paid us the equivalent of my pension for one year and when we went to the bank we couldn't believe it. I asked Monsieur Vincent for more time, as I sense that I will only be able to work bit by bit because of the acid vapors from the engraving plates. If it was hard for me to stand it before, it will now be even more so because of my general weakness from the pleurisy. I had pneumonia, Chatito—I didn't want to tell you so as not to worry you. I have now recovered and this visit to *Floréal* lifted my spirits again. It gives me the opportunity to make more money so I can join you, and just the thought of it is like a preview of paradise. I didn't dare ask for an advance (a monetary one, of course) but Monsieur Vincent spontaneously offered one to me. I wanted to throw my arms around him; instead I limited myself to thanking him in the most courteous way I could. He seems to be a man who deeply understands human

nature and regards it with indulgence. I
think the great satisfaction I experience
when I sit down at my work table—or better
said, your work table—and begin working
on my projects compensates for my pres-
ent dearth of funds. Thanks to Monsieur
Vincent, I will now have some money to buy
coal and I'll add four or five potatoes to my
filet à provisions. In the last few months my
economic situation has deteriorated so much
that I attended the Russian Easter celebration
just for the hard-boiled eggs and enormous
loaves of bread they pass out. They gave me
two eggs, and an old man without teeth and
with a fur coat also gave me his, assuring
me that he didn't like them. So, I got to the
house with a huge loaf of bread and four
hard-boiled eggs, enough to feed me for
four days. I even went to the Rue Darru and
bought pickles. Do you remember how much
you loved the barrels of herring, the black
olives, the piroshkis, the sausages, the onions,

the kulibiak, those pickles that are so good
for a hangover? At home I made tea and ate
slowly, delighting in the first hard-boiled
egg . . . You should have seen the incredible
icons they take out once a year after having
them hidden away for a lifetime! There isn't
a single Russian who leaves Saint Petersburg without his samovar and his icon. The
procession of icons went around the church
while the most violent and startling chorus
I have ever heard burst forth from inside. I
can still see the midnight mass with the
transition from songs of grief to those of
resurrection and triumph, the faces of the
people in the procession lit from below by
the candles they carried, the women with
their trays of painted eggs, their Easter pas-
tries of fresh cheese and others called *kulich*
that people bring to be blessed. But I was
most touched by the hugs from unknowns
who took me into their arms and gave me
big, noisy kisses on my cheeks. I needed

that, Diego, I needed to feel human warmth.
I no longer ask for wisdom or strength,
just a little warmth, that they let me warm
myself by their fire. I would have loved to
go to La Ville de Petrograd where everyone went to listen to balalaikas and Gypsy
songs. I miss Russian food, just biting into
a hard-boiled egg brings back my childhood.
Do you remember that beggar who always
stood in front of the cathedral, drunk at
no matter what time of day, and when you
walked by he would put out his hand and
say in Russian, "Give me something for a
little vodka," and he seemed to you to be the
most convincing man in the world? I didn't
see him and I missed him, I asked about him
in the store but they don't know anything.
It's one more absence in my life. What ever
made me get sick and not go out of the house
for so long? On my way back I saw the dirty
black houses that you used to observe so
thoroughly. I went into the little damp

courtyard which is also black and looked at the lighted windows, and I made a sketch. I learned from you to take notes, to express myself instead of brooding in silence, to move, to draw every day, to do, speak instead of meditate, not hide the commotion, and I feel so strong from this abundant activity, this sense of expansion and plenitude. If I could, I would have drawn the Russian choir in all its splendor. I drew a few of the wax faces in the darkness of the church and I sense that they are strangely alive. I returned along the *quais*. The clear water reflected the clear firmament. The *péniches* were the only black things and they darkened the water with their shadows. Every once in a while a boat would tow one along and then let it drop farther up, I never understood why. Then I was overtaken by a sensation of pure religious exaltation, the same as I used to feel when I was young in Saint Petersburg, after midnight supper

when the masters and servants would kiss
and hug one another and I would stay in
my room unable to sleep, looking at the
curtains I had washed and ironed with the
servants, and the icon in the corner with the
candle that softly illuminated the Byzantine
Virgin. Then I would pray, full of love with
no object because I had no one to love. Does
my love now have an object? I miss you, my
Chatito, I raise my sketch in the air and
show it to you. I ask myself if you are eating
well, who takes care of you, if you still keep
up those exhausting days of work, if your
fits of rage have diminished—an inspired
rage, productive and creative when you
would, like a river, drag yourself along, spin
yourself around, and hurl yourself down as
we followed, lost in the rapids. I wonder if
you live only to paint as you did here in
Paris, if you love a new woman, what path
you have taken. If this is true, Diego, tell me,
I would know how to understand, haven't

==

I always been able to understand everything? Sometimes I think it would be better
to leave Montparnasse, abandon the Rue du
Départ, never go back to La Rotonde, break
with the past, but as long as I don't hear
from you I am paralyzed. Just a few lines
would save me days and nights of anguish.
I hug you, Diego, with the agitation you so
often viewed with tenderness,

Your Quiela

P.S. I am going to send you the sketches of
the engravings one by one in a cardboard
envelope so that you can check them out
and make some suggestions. Without you, I
feel fragile even in my work.

$\mathcal{D}$ECEMBER 29 · 1921

I regret not having started to paint when I was younger, and now that so much time has gone by I miss those years at the University of Saint Petersburg when I first took up drawing. At the beginning, my father would come fetch me. I can still hear our footsteps echoing through the empty streets, and we would talk as we walked home and he would ask me how I was getting along, if I was intimidated by having men in my night painting class. After seeing how much confidence I had and how kind my classmates were, he let me walk home alone. He was so proud when I won the scholarship to the Academy of Fine Arts in Saint Petersburg!

From the very first day I walked into the atelier in Paris, I worked out a schedule that only you would find acceptable: from eight o'clock to twelve-thirty, from one-thirty to five o'clock in the afternoon and then again from eight to ten o'clock at night. Painting nine hours a day! Can you imagine what that is like? Yes, you can imagine it, you who live only to paint. I ate, thinking about how I would manage the shadows of the faces I had just seen, I dined as fast as I could, remembering the painting left on the easel. When I did encaustic exercises I thought about the moment I would return and open the door of the studio and find that familiar and persistent scent of lavender. I even went to the laboratory at the university to research the chemical and physical properties of paint. I melted my own wax with a blowtorch for the encaustic, and then I would add the lavender essence and pig-

....

ments, and once in a while the students would come over and ask me, "How's the color coming?" At lunchtime I would get angry if anybody talked to me, distracting me from thinking about the next line I would draw that I wanted to be fluid and pure and exact. I was possessed, Diego, and I was only twenty years old. I was never tired, on the contrary, I would have died if anyone had forced me to give up that life. I avoided the theater, I avoided going out, I avoided other people's company because the amount of pleasure I got from these things was so much less than the intense pleasure I felt from learning my trade. My fellow students were jealous because of all the praise André Lhote lavished on me. Once he paused in front of a head viewed from beneath and asked me:

"Did you do this alone?"

"Yes."

"How long have you been here?"

"Ten days."

A Danish, a Spanish, and a French girl who had been studying for three years came closer to listen.

"You have an extraordinary talent."

"Would you like to see another bust, maestro?"

"Show me everything you have done, immediately. I want to see every line you have ever drawn."

I took everything out and the others gathered around. I looked at the Spanish girl, who drew admirably (she did noteworthy studies with magnificent models and even went to the Louvre to copy), and a shadow seemed to come over her eyes as he spoke, she went pale, while my cheeks were burning red with pleasure. Lhote encouraged me so much that I even went on Saturdays and in the evening, and the director would look at me affectionately. "Mademoiselle Bielova, you are magnificent. You work while everyone else is resting or having fun." "I have nothing else to do, monsieur." To find me on Sunday, all you had to do was open the door of the atelier. On Sunday I would go up to Saint-Cloud, Diego, I always liked to walk there under the fruit trees in the middle of the green field with my sketchbook. I was like a photographer with a pencil instead of a camera. I filled three-quarters of the booklet with sketches and in the corner of one of the pages I still have my *Emploi du Temps*, and it makes me smile because I divided the twenty-four hours of the day so that I had five hours to sleep, one hour to get dressed and bathe (while I cursed the water that froze in the pipes and had to be heated up on the stove), two hours for three meals a day (not for my sake but for Aunt Natasha's, who would scold me for not visiting her, for not listening to her, for not taking good care of myself, for not getting fresh air, for not going with her to the market and visiting), and sixteen hours to paint. The trip to and from the studio seemed so slow, Diego! If I could have, I would have slept next to my easel, every minute lost was one less minute to paint. I wanted to do four years' worth of work in one year, be better than everyone else, win the Prix de Rome. My vehemence upset Aunt Natasha. One night I said I would go with her to the theater, but when I saw all those people going in with those expectant, empty faces waiting to be entertained, I thought, "What am I doing here instead of in front of my easel?" and without further hesitation I turned around and left my aunt in the middle of the foyer. The next morning she didn't want to let me into her house. I could not understand why. I didn't remember anything. I think painting is like that, you forget everything, you lose all sense of time, of other people, of obligations, of daily life that spins around you without your even noticing it. In the atelier one afternoon, I was walking over to the other side of the room to get a bottle of gasoline to clean my palette and I heard the Spanish girl saying very clearly so that I would hear her, "Everyone always makes ex-tra-or-di-na-ry, phe-no-me-nal, pro-di-gious progress at first. Everyone impresses the maestros. The hard part comes afterwards, when you lose the impunity and freshness and daring of the first sketches and you fully realize how much more there is to learn, that in fact you really don't know

anything." I kept on walking. My palette
was clean and the Danish girl, who is so
nice, surely thought I was hurt, because she
helped me arrange my still life—the glass,
the three oranges, the spoon set in the glass
just right so it cast the perfect shadow on
the folded napkin, the slice of bread. I wasn't
hurt, but the Spanish girl's words rang in
my ears and at night I could not sleep,
thinking, "What if suddenly I lose this ease?
If suddenly I get stuck because I realize I
do not know anything? If suddenly I become paralyzed by self-criticism or if I use
up all my talent?" It would have been like
losing my soul, Diego, because I lived only
to paint, I saw everything as a prospective
drawing—a skirt blowing in the breeze, a
worker's rugged hands as he sat by me eating, a loaf of bread, a bottle of wine, the
coppery reflection of a woman's hair, the
leaves, the first sprouts of a young tree. For
example, I never stopped to look at a child

in the street for the sake of the child him-
self. I saw him already as a line on the
paper, I had to be able to capture the purity
of his chin, the roundness of his little head,
his pug nose—why do little children always
have pug noses, Chatito?—that sweet mouth
that is never still. And I had to do it all as
quickly as possible because children never
stand still for even five minutes. But I never
saw the child, I saw his line, his shapes, his
lights, I wouldn't even ask him his name.
By the way, do you remember that middle-
aged Belgian model who could sleep with
her eyes open?

Now everything has changed and I feel
sad when I watch the children crossing the
street on their way to school. They are not
drawings, they are children of flesh and
blood. I ask myself if they are dressed
warmly, if their mothers put a nutritious
goûter, maybe *un petit pain au chocolat*, in

their knapsacks. I think that one of them
could be our little boy and I feel that I
would give—I don't know what—my work,
my life as a painter, just to see him like that
with his blue-and-white *tablier d'écolier*, to
have dressed him, brushed his hair, told him
not to get ink all over his fingers, not to tear
his uniform, not to . . . well, anything those
lucky mothers do who at this very moment
in every house in Paris are waiting for their
children to return so they can take them in
their arms. Life takes its toll, Diego, it de-
pletes us of exactly that which we believe
to be the source of our vitality: our work.
Not only have I lost my son, but I have also
lost my creativity. I do not know how to
paint any more, I do not want to paint any
more. Now that I am able to paint at home,
I do not take advantage of the time. This has
been a long winter, it gets dark at four
o'clock in the afternoon, and then I have to
stop working for one or two hours while my

eyes get adjusted to the electric light. Do you remember when you said that blue eyes are blue because they never managed to acquire any color, that the women in your country are brown and that this color is forthright and definitive like mud, a plowed field, wood? I feel as if these faded eyes are weaker now, and it is very difficult for me to train them to look at the blank page, to focus them. I sit in front of the table with a blanket over my legs, because it is the only way not to fall asleep, and I begin slowly, painfully. Now that I would like to have an Aunt Natasha to visit, she is dead and I do not know who to turn to. Good-bye, Diego, excuse me, your Angelina, who tonight, in spite of the work for *Floréal* awaiting her on the table, is demoralized. I hug you and tell you once again that I love you, I will always love you, no matter what happens.

Your Quiela

$\mathcal{J}$ANUARY 2 · 1 9 2 2

On one of the sheets of paper on the table,
instead of the usual sketches, I have written
in a handwriting I don't even recognize, "It
is six o'clock in the morning and Diego is
not here." On another piece of paper that I
would never dare use for anything other
than to draw, I am surprised to see my
scribble: "It is eight o'clock in the morning.
I do not hear Diego making noise, going to
the bathroom, walking down the hallway
to the window and slowly and deliberately
looking up at the sky as I am so used to and
I think I am going to go crazy," and on the
same piece of paper, a little farther down
the page: "It is eleven o'clock in the morning. I am a bit crazed. Diego is definitely
not here, I think he will never come and I

::

pace around the room like someone who has
lost her mind. I have nothing to keep me
busy, I cannot work on the engravings. Today I do not want to be sweet, calm, decent,
submissive, understanding, and resigned—
all those qualities of mine my friends always praise. I do not want to be maternal,
either; Diego is not just a grown-up child,
Diego is a man who does not write because
he does not love me any more and has completely forgotten me." The last few words
were written with violence, I almost tore the
paper with the pen, and now I am crying at
my childish self-indulgence. When did I
write that? Yesterday? The day before yesterday? Last night? Four nights ago? I don't
know, I cannot remember. But now, Diego,
as I look at my rantings and ravings I ask
you—and this is perhaps the most serious
question I have ever asked in my life—do
you not love me any more, Diego? I want
you to tell me sincerely. You have had plenty

::

of time to think about it and come to a deci-
sion, at least unconsciously, even if you have
not had the opportunity to put it into words.
Now is the time to do so. If you don't, we
will simply get to a point of useless suffering, useless and monotonous like a toothache
and with the same results. The fact is that
you do not write me, that you will write me
less and less if we let more time go by, and
after a few years we will meet as strangers
—that is, if we ever see each other again. As
far as I am concerned, I can tell you that the
toothache will continue until the root is
rotten, so don't you think it would be better
to pull it out if there is nothing left that
draws you to me? Every once in a while I
receive the money orders you send, but each
time your messages are shorter, more im-
personal, and in the last one you did not
write a single word. Your "I am well, hope
you are too, regards, Diego" nourishes me
indefinitely, and as I look at your beloved

handwriting I try to discover some hidden meaning, but the bareness of those quickly written lines leaves little to the imagination. I hang on to the words "hope you are too" and think, "Diego wants me to be well," but my euphoria does not last very long because there is nothing to sustain it. I suppose I should understand by all this that you do not love me any more, but I cannot accept it. Every once in a while I get this terrible sense of foreboding, but I try to rid myself of it at all cost. I bathe myself in cold water to get rid of the birds of ill omen that flutter around inside me, I go outside to take a walk, I feel cold, I try to keep active when in fact I am delirious. I take refuge in the past, I reflect on our first meetings when, dizzy with joy and tension, I would wait for you. I used to think that from among this multitude, in the middle of the day from the Boulevard Raspail, no, from Montparnasse, from among all these

men and women who pour out of the Métro
and walk up the stairs, he is going to appear . . . no, he will never appear because
he is only a product of my imagination, so
in the meantime I will sit here in this café
in front of this round table and no matter
how much I strain my eyes, no matter how
fast my heart beats, I will never see anybody
who looks even remotely like Diego. I would
tremble, Diego, I couldn't even bring the
cup to my lips. How could you possibly walk
through the streets like a common mortal!
You would always approach from the same
direction. Only a miracle could make you
emerge from that throng of people with
their heads bent, dark and faceless figures,
and come over to me with your head up and
that smile of yours that makes me warm all
over just thinking of it. You would sit down
next to me as if nothing had happened, unaware of how anxiously I had been awaiting
you, and you would turn around to look at

the Indian reading the London *Times* and the Arab who cleaned his nails with his fork. I can still see you with your unshined shoes, your old rumpled hat, your wrinkled pants, your monumental stature, your protruding stomach, and I think that nobody, absolutely nobody can show off such shoddy clothes as majestically as you do. I would burn inside as I listened to you, as you caressed my thighs with your passionate hands, I could not even swallow and yet I would seem so calm and you would comment, "How calm you are, Angelina, how peaceful, how well your name suits you, when I say it I can hear a slight rustle of wings!" I felt drugged. You occupied all my thoughts, and I was terribly afraid of disappointing you. I wanted to send you a note that very night, rewriting the scene of our meeting, because I would go over in my head every sentence we spoke and feel

ashamed of my awkwardness, my nervous-
ness, my silences. I would try to imagine an
ideal meeting after which you would go
back to your work with the certainty that I
was worthy of your attentions. I trembled,
Diego, I was very conscious of my feelings
and my inarticulate desire. I had so much
to tell you—I spent the whole day repeating
to myself the words I would say to you—
and then when I would see you I couldn't
utter a word, and at night I would sob into
my pillow, biting my lip. "Tomorrow he
will not come to meet me, surely tomorrow
he will not come. What possible interest
could he have in me?" And the next afternoon, there I was in front of my round mar-
ble table, in between the Spaniard who, like
me, was always looking out onto the street,
and the Turk who emptied the whole sugar
bowl into his coffee, both of them unaware
of my desperation, of the cup trembling in

my hands, of my eyes devouring the grey and anonymous multitude that passed by and out of which you would emerge and walk towards me.

Do you love me, Diego? Yes, it is painful, but absolutely necessary for me to know. You see, Diego, my personality, my habits, in short, my entire being, went through a complete transformation during the years we spent together: I became completely Mexican, and I feel connected *par procuration* to your language, your country, to thousands of little things, and I feel much less foreign with you than in any other country. I cannot even consider returning to my homeland, not so much because of the political events but because I cannot identify with my fellow Russians. On the other hand, I feel so comfortable with your people, so at ease in their presence.

Our Mexican friends are the ones who have led me to believe I could make a living in Mexico giving lessons.

But these are, after all, only secondary issues. The most important thing is that I can make no plans to travel to your country if you no longer have any feelings for me and if the mere idea of my presence makes you uncomfortable. If this were not the case, I might even be able to help you—I could mix your colors, prepare your stencils, help you as I did when we were together in Spain and France during the war. This is why I am asking you, Diego, to clarify your intentions. This week, my friendship with the Mexican painters in Paris has been a great source of strength to me, especially Ángel Zárraga, who is so soft-spoken, so discreet he is almost shy. When I am with them, I feel as if I were in Mexico and just

::

a bit closer to you, even though they are less
expressive, more reserved, not as free as you
are. Whirlwinds seemed to arise in your
wake. I remember one time Zadkin asked
me, "Is he drunk?" Your intoxication came
from your images, your words, your colors,
you would speak and all of us would listen
to you in disbelief. For me, you yourself
were a whirlwind, besides the ecstasy I felt
when I was in your presence; when I was
with you I felt as if I possessed at least a
small piece of the world. The other day Élie
Faure said that a spring of legends from a
supernatural world had dried up since you
left and that we Europeans were in need of
this new mythology because poetry, fantasy,
sensitive intelligence, and spiritual dyna-
mism were dead in Europe. We miss all those
fables you invented about the sun and the
first inhabitants of the world, your myth-
ologies, the plumed-serpent space ship that
once existed and flew through the skies and

landed in Mexico. Now we have forgotten how to behold the world with that greed, that ardent rebelliousness, that tropical rage; we are so much more evasive, more inhibited, more concealed. I have never been able to reveal myself the way you do; every gesture of yours is creative; it is new, as if you were a newborn, an untouchable man, so full of that great and uncanny purity, so virginal. I once said this to Bakst and he said you came from a country that also has just been born. "He is a savage," he said, "and savages have not been contaminated by our decadent ci-vi-li-za-tion. But you must be careful, because they have been known to devour small white women in one gulp." Can't you tell how strong your presence is among us, Diego? As you can see, we are sad. Élie Faure said he has written to you and has received no reply. What are you doing in Mexico, Diego, what are you painting? Many of our friends have dispersed.

....

Marie Blanchard went to Brujas again to paint and she wrote to tell me that she tried to rent the room in the same house in which we were so happy, when we had so much fun together, when you would wake up at dawn to worship the sun, and the women, carrying their baskets of tomatoes on their way to the market, would lift their arms in the air and cross themselves when they saw you standing there totally naked in the window. Juan Gris wants to go to Mexico and is counting on you for help, you promised you would speak to the director of the Cultural Institute of Mexico for him. Ortiz de Zárate and Ángel Zárraga are planning to stay around here for a while. Lipschitz also mentioned that he might travel but I have lost track of him lately because he stopped visiting me. Picasso went south to search for the sun. I have heard nothing from the Zetings, as I told you before. Sometimes I think it is better this way. Hayden,

when I told him how often I write to you,
spread out his arms and said, "But Angelina,
how long do you think it takes a letter to get
there? It takes a long time, one, two, maybe
three months, and if you write to Diego every
eight or fifteen days, as you said, you don't
give him enough time to answer." That
made me feel a bit better, not altogether,
but I sort of thought that nature might be
conspiring against us. Nevertheless, it seems
futile to remind you that there are ships
that travel from France to Mexico. Zadkin,
on the other hand, said something terrible to
me as he put his arm around me and forced
me to walk by his side: "Angelina, don't you
realize that love cannot be forced through
compassion?"

My dear Diego, with all my strength, I
embrace you desperately across the ocean
that separates us.

Your Quiela

ℐANUARY 17 · 1922

You have said nothing about the sketches, so I have begun work on them alone because *Floréal* cannot be kept waiting. At first I was doing still lifes, bottles and fruits, curved lines, circles of color over an angular table to break the roundness, because in the last few months my figures have not been geometric but round and soft instead. I can't seem to get rid of straight lines as I used to, I keep them encircled in a blue light, the same light you said encircled me whenever I came into your view. Afterwards, and without even thinking about it, I began to paint urban landscapes, and then all of a sudden I was painting children's heads and faces that are in my opinion the best I've

done so far. I have my son at my very finger-
tips. I painted a one-and-a-half-year-old
child with his head to one side and a painful
expression on his face, almost transparent, a
bit like the way you painted me four years
ago, and I like it a lot. My colors are not
brilliant. They are pale, and of course the
most convincing are the different tones of
blue. You see, in spite of everything I have
been working. It is my métier. I complain,
but my hand flows, the paint flows softly.
And all the while, your voice rings in my
ears: "Play, Angelina, play, play as Picasso
told you to. Don't take everything so ser-
iously," and I try to lighten my hand, to let
the brush dance, I even let go of it and shake
my hand like a puppet and I remember your
Mexican game, "Tengo manita, no tengo
manita, porque la tengo desconchavadita,"
and I return to the canvas and am unable to
play because I feel my dead son in between

my fingers. Nevertheless, I believe I have achieved a kind of secret vibration, a rare transparency.

A few Russian friends I knew during the war, Archipenko and Larionov, came by but I did not go with them to La Rotonde. It is too upsetting for me, and since I cannot offer them anything to eat, not even vodka, they soon leave. They see the blank piece of paper on the table and they say good-bye respectfully. "We do not want to take up your time, you are working." Zadkin, on the other hand, asked me the other day where your drawings were and he started looking through them. I took out the unsigned oil painting that looks like *El despertador* and he told me that Rosenberg might be interested in it. He told me that Ilya Ehrenburg had sold him a painting of yours for 280 francs, that Rosenberg had a good eye and bought avidly. "You don't have to be so

::

broke, Angelina. Why don't you sell some of these? I am sure you have not even tried." I told him that I would not, that they were my life's blood and that they will be the only things I carry with me when I go to Mexico. He shook his head and asked me again, "Why don't you put the samovar on the stove?" I told him I had lost the habit. "Don't you have any tea?" "No." So he went out and came back with an aluminum box from the Rue Darru and said, "Now we are going to have tea." He has an affected and brusque way of doing things, but it doesn't make me feel bad, not even when he stands in front of one of your sketches and speaks about the disturbing and arbitrary force of the lines. "It is as if he fills all the empty spaces, he does not know what silence is," he shouted. "On the contrary," I said, and I told him how silent you always became before creating. It was the first time I spoke for any length of time without stop-

▪▪▪

ping, at least it seemed like a long time to me, and Zadkin observed me in silence and then said, shaking his head, "You have become so Mexican that you have forgotten how to make tea." He is right. I managed to make the tea turn out badly. Ossip Zadkin left at nine o'clock in the evening. His rosy cheeks and bristly hair make me happy, his rapid and abrupt gestures and his goodness. I was happy when I went to bed because I had drunk tea, because I had spoken about you, because his friendship is so comforting to me.

Diego, I embrace you with all my soul, I love you so much.

Your Quiela

I heard through friends that you are also sending money to Marievna Vorobiev Stebelska (and I do admire your generosity), but today, so I would no longer have any doubts, you sent three hundred francs to me to give to her, begging with that rapid scrawl of yours that I make sure she gets them because, as you say, I am the most responsible person in the world. *C'est un peu fort*, don't you think, Diego? I asked Fischer to give her the money. I have not seen them again, neither Marievna nor little Marika, but people say she looks very much like you. Even though I am grateful that you chose me as your confidante, I cannot see them because when I do, I become very jealous and I cannot repress how I feel. You were right to tell me, Diego, I do not reproach you for that. After all, it was Ehrenburg who introduced you to Marievna in La Rotonde, when you asked, "Who is that attractive Caucasian woman?" At that time Marievna also wanted to be my friend, but I am so fiercely jealous I cannot stand to think about either the mother or the daughter. When I asked you for another child, even though you were leaving, even though you were returning to Mexico without me, you refused. And Marievna has your daughter and she is alive and growing up and looks like you, even though you call her "the daughter of the armistice." You have been my lover, my son, my inspiration, my god; you are my homeland. I feel Mexican, my language is Spanish even though I make a mess of it when I speak it. If you do not return, if you do not send for me, I will not only lose you but I will also lose myself and all that I could have been. You were only one among many to Marievna. You yourself said as much: "It was only because of the armistice. All the women opened up their arms to the men in the wild excitement of the end of the war. In this way, life avenged death." Marievna Vorobiev Stebelska spent all her time with our Russian friends, sitting in La Rotonde with Boris Svinkov. One night she said, almost screaming, that she had been Gorki's lover; we all thought she was Ehrenburg's lover. In Montparnasse she always called attention to herself by the uninhibited way she would walk over to us. During that period, I had no time to spare for Marievna. You were the only thing that interested me, how you got along with my friends, how at first you would listen with such intense concentration, and then, in the heat of the discussion, scream your ideas at them in Spanish with a few French and Russian words thrown in. You invented your own language, twisting it at your will and breaking the boundaries. Your ideas went beyond the limitations of language. Your clarity was stunning, especially to me, and I took classes to learn your language, studying day after day, going over the grammar with the diligence of a schoolgirl, and I still never dared to speak it. I remember so well how our friends' eyes were riveted on you! And Marievna's eyes, as she watched you in wonderment. Simply because she admired you, I became friends with her and you got her pregnant, and in spite of that you and I carried on. I knew that our friends felt sympathy for me, not for Marievna. She was your lover, I was your wife. You fell ill because of your relationship with her. We went to Périgueux for the oyster cure, and afterwards you wanted to go on a diet of strawberries. You and I went through the same hardships together. You told me everything: about Marievna's insanity, her feverish pursuit of you, how dangerous she was. I listened and shared everything; Marievna was my torment as well as yours.

We shared everything, Diego. When there was a piece of cheese, a loaf of bread, a bottle of wine, we would call our friends to come over and enjoy these delicacies with us. Do you remember the sausage I bought on the black market and how Modigliani ate almost the entire thing? And when Hayden carried the Camembert in the pleats of his coat and almost dropped it from the window as he leaned out? What days those were, Chatito! We laughed like children while surrounded by such horror! Do you remember when Adam Fischer brought *un litre de gros rouge* to the house and on the way he couldn't wait so he took a sip and another one at the corner and another one at the door of the studio and he was drunk when he arrived because it had been so long since he had had anything to drink? Marievna

was part of our group and in a way she be-
trayed us all. Last Thursday I followed the
children—sometimes I surprise myself fol-
lowing the *écoliers*—and sat down with them
in the Jardin du Luxembourg to see the
Guignol. One of the puppets was a tall
woman who had a blond wig with bangs
that came down over her blue eyes, and it
reminded me of Marievna. She did the same
things in the play that Marievna used to do,
she went around slapping everybody in the
face, which made the audience explode with
laughter. She was like a wild beast. All the
other puppets communicated by talking to
each other, while she just went around hit-
ting everyone. The children began calling
to her. They wanted to see her beat up
anyone who crossed her path. She was very
popular. So was Marievna. Even with me.
But enough of Marievna! Do you remember
that flask full of beach sand we brought
back from Mallorca, Cala, and San Vicente

and how you spread the sand over the canvas, leaving its texture intact? I have not been able to find it anywhere and it pains me because I remember your excitement when you were by the Mediterranean and how the water played around our feet. I want to find it because I just painted a water landscape and would like to be able to capture something from that beach.

I am progressing slowly. I am very far from being able to paint as the bird sings, as Renoir said. But I am a bird after all and I have nested forever in your hands.

Your Quiela

A letter finally arrived from Mexico. I opened it anxiously, it was from Papa, I love him so much. It pained me greatly to know that he was ill and I am truly sorry that I cannot see him, but as far as my desire to see all of you goes, I will no longer mention it, Diego, because you must take the initiative and if you do not . . . it is really so tedious for me to keep on insisting. Right now I am thinking that I could be by Papa's side, taking care of him, returning some of the love and affection he sends me in his letters. I wrote back immediately and asked him about Mexico, about your mother and her overwhelming workload, about the house, your sister María, about what you are doing, and I trust he will write me back because in the few lines he wrote I could feel the great warmth of his heart. I am exalted by the fact that your father calls me his *daughter*. He thinks I am your wife, he *knows* I am your wife, so this means there is no other, only me, and this is a great comfort to me, Diego, in spite of your silence that is probably due to the excess of work, to the changes, the projects you are working on, your long afternoon discussions. I imagine you sitting around a table sharing your ideas, shaking people up, forcing them to think, arousing them with your passion, angering them, and then exploding in rage as you exploded when I told you I was pregnant. You shouted and threatened to throw yourself from the seventh floor, and you went crazy and screamed at me as you unlatched the window, "If that child bothers me, I am going to throw him out this window." From that moment on you began to live like someone possessed, as if you wanted to compress an entire lifetime into one hour. You painted for twenty hours, leaving only four hours for sleep, you were so feverish you began to talk to yourself. And then I called the doctor and he told you, "The lady is pregnant, not you." You protested, "How are we going to bring a child into this inhumane world? How can I change the world with my painting before he is born?" You told me about the French soldiers who deserted or revolted because they didn't want to fight any more and those who carried on only because they had been threatened with the firing squad, and you repeated incessantly that to bear a child was like committing infanticide. You tortured me with this idea as I tortured you with my pregnancy. But I wanted to bear a child, your child and mine. Other women took care of him, but he was my child and soon I would have been able to bring him back with me to the studio, as soon as he stopped letting out those moans that grated so much on your nerves. Winter came. I still hear people say, "Ah, the winter of 1917!" The child died, but you and I survived the hardships. Apollinaire died a year later. Once I heard you say, "Apollinaire and my child died of the same thing: human stupidity." I remember a poem by Apollinaire. I will transcribe it for you here:

> *In short, oh laughing ones, you have taken nothing so great from mankind; you have just barely extracted a bit of fat from his misery; but those of us who die from living far away from one another stretch out our arms and a long cargo train glides over those rails.*

That was when you began to say it was inconceivable that humanity would con-

....

tinue to tolerate a system that produced insanities like war. You would shout again and again that a solution would soon be found. You held many discussions with the Russians—my revolutionary emigrant friends—about the role of painting in the future social order. Every day we waited for our friends to return from the front. And that was when I realized you had *le mal du pays*. You would turn your eyes towards the pale sun and remember another one, and deep down you already wanted to leave. You were fed up. You were disgusted with Europe and its great war, the cold, the muddy troops returning with their belongings, and Apollinaire, unrecognizable in death with his head bandaged, a splinter in his skull; everything disgusted you. It was time for you to leave. The only thing that might have detained you was your son and he was lying beneath the snow. I would have taken off with you but there was only enough money for that one ticket. I no longer received my allowance from Saint Petersburg; the war interrupted everything. Essentially the war had broken your ties to France and, when our son died, your ties to me as well. I felt it, Diego, and I accepted it. I firmly believed I would join you later on, that those ten years we spent together had not been spent in vain, after all I had been your wife and I am sure you loved me. I only have to look at the portrait you drew of me to feel your tenderness. I can see it in the tilt of my head, in the softness of the arched eyebrows, in the wide forehead, as if you wanted to express the intelligence and sensitivity you perceived in me. The wondering eyes suggest an admiration for life; the thoughtful mouth has a faint smile. I see the three Angelinas—before, during, and after the pregnancy. I see my swollen belly you lingered over dotingly. "Diego, son," you wrote, and in another corner of the canvas, "Sweet Angelina."

One time you told me, "Here, all is light faces against a dark background. In my country, all is dark faces against a light background." Now I know you said that because you missed the light that penetrates the retina, but at the time I thought you were saying it because I was so transparent, so diaphanous. One day you said, "You are so pale, you are almost translucent. I can see your heart." Another day, when I came and sat down in front of you, you lifted your eyes and I heard you say, "How wonderfully white your face is. It always seems to emerge from the darkness." I thought you were en- amored of whiteness until one morning you surprised me by saying, "Juan Gris is the only mulatto here and he denies it by claim- ing he is Spanish. The good in him is the black part of him and the bad in him is the white part of him. He tries to pass for a Spaniard because Parisians look down on Spanish-Americans. How much those pale, wrinkled Europeans would like to be able to walk with the catlike grace of the tropics, how they long for one ray of sun to ignite and redden their insipid and languid skins! How old, dusty, and rusty Europe is!" I was hurt. I tried not to be and yet I couldn't help but take it personally. Europe had pushed you over the edge with its ration-ings, its stale black bread, its fatigue, and its soot and you would complain more and more frequently: "How dismal the factory sirens are! Industrialization is so sad and macabre! In my country, people sit down to eat in a slow and formal manner as gods should."

I often think you neither write nor send money for my ticket because you are afraid of facing the difficulties and complications of living *à deux* in Mexico. I have thought about this a great deal and I believe that in your country, where we have never lived together, we could build a life for ourselves in such a way that we would not give each other more than what could be given spontaneously. As always, you would be working and my drawing classes and portraits would keep me busy. I would make money however possible so I would not be at home most of the day, and we would see each other in the evenings. Our relationship would be built on a foundation of work and mutual good will, of camaraderie and independence. I don't think I ever interfered with your independence, Diego, never, not even with Marievna, don't you remember how I accepted it when you told me about her? I always tried to make your life easier so that you could paint in spite of our poverty. Even now I would be satisfied to mix your colors, clean your palette, keep your brushes in perfect condition, be your helper, and I would not get pregnant. Here in Paris our life was very difficult. There, under the Mexican sun, perhaps it would be less so and I would try to be a good woman for you. Once you said, "Quiela, you have been a good woman for me. By your side, I can work as if I were alone. You never interfered and I will be grateful to you for the rest of my life for that." I will not bother you in Mexico either, Diego, I promise you. Ever since I left Saint Petersburg, I have known how to make it on my own. Even you called me *débrouil-larde* in French slang when I would show up with a kilo of potatoes or a half a pound of cream and I would make rice a la mexicana that you devoured in a second. My parents taught me that I must only count on myself and I will forever be indebted to them for this; I shall never stop appreciating their gift to me. I come from one of those middle-class families that were the fountainhead of Russian liberalism and radicalism, and my parents insisted upon my having a profession. Just as if I had been a boy, I had to prepare myself, study, get training, learn how to work. How wise they were! They gave me the key to my own happiness. The greatest source of satisfaction in my life has been the fact that I have achieved economic independence, and I am proud of being one of the most advanced women of my time. Even when I was expelled from the Academy of Fine Arts for participating in the student strike, my parents did not lose faith in me. They did not even reproach me, and when the director readmitted me, they looked at me with the pride I always saw in their eyes and commented: "It couldn't have turned out differently. Angelina was right and justice is being done." When my parents died, I knew that the only way to respect their memory was to continue my career and so I came to Paris to study. Many

of us Russians arrived at the Gare du Nord.
Diaghilev traveled the same day I did and
Zadkin came on the train the day before.
Almost one Russian a day arrived, all eager,
expectant Russians, bewildered by the splendor of Paris. With my modest inheritance
I was able to rent a studio apartment with
a tiny bathroom and a smaller kitchen without ventilation, but I was better off than
many of my fellow Russians. Soon afterwards my Aunt Natasha came, my only
relative in Paris, and she invited me every
week to have, according to her, "at least
one decent meal," and she would give me
strength to continue "that crazy artistic life
you lead."

I met you at La Rotonde, Diego, and it
was love at first sight. I was interested in
you the minute I saw you enter, so tall, with
your wide-brimmed hat, your fiery eyes and
friendly smile. I heard Zadkin say, "Here
comes the Mexican cowboy," and some

others chimed in, "Voilà l'exotique." Your six-foot-three frame filled the entire doorway, your unkempt curly beard, your sweet face, and above all, those clothes of yours that seemed about to burst at the seams any moment, the dirty and wrinkled clothes of a man who doesn't have a woman to look after him. But the goodness in your eyes made the greatest impression on me. I could perceive a magnetic atmosphere that encircled you, something the others felt only later. Everyone was interested in you, in the ideas you expressed so impetuously, your chaotic outbursts of joy. I still remember how you looked at me with surprise and tenderness. When we got up from the table and stood there together, Zadkin exclaimed, "Look how funny they look together: the Mexican savage, enormous and flamboyant, and that sweet, tiny creature enveloped in a light blue haze!" Very naturally, without vows or dowries, without economic agreements or contracts, we came together. Neither of us believed in those bourgeois institutions. We faced life together and we spent ten years that way, the ten best years of my life. If I could be born again, I would once again choose to have spent those ten years with you, full of so much pain and happiness, Diego. I am still your bluebird, I am still simply blue as you always said. I bend down my head, my pained head, and put it on your shoulder and kiss you on your neck, Diego, Diego, Diego, who I love so much.

Your Quiela

It seems as though ages have gone by since I last wrote to you or heard anything from you, Diego. I have not wanted to write because it is so difficult for me to remain silent about certain things I am carrying around in my heart and which I am absolutely certain are useless to discuss. I pick up my pen only because I feel it would be rude not to thank you for the money you sent me. I have not thanked you for the last three money orders of February 6, March 10, and the beginning of June for 260, 297, and 300 francs respectively, and by now more than four months have gone by. I did send you the new engravings that appeared in *Floréal*, but have received no response from you. If I told you I would have preferred a note rather than the money, I would be only partially lying; it is true I would prefer your love, but thanks to the money I have been able to survive. My economic situation is extremely precarious and I have even considered giving up painting, surrendering, finding a job as a teacher, a typist, or anything else for eight hours a day, an all-round *abrutissement*, going to the movies and the theater on Saturdays and taking a walk in Saint-Cloud or Robinson on Sundays. But I do not want to do that. I am willing to carry on under these conditions so long as I can devote myself to painting and accept the consequences: poverty, grief, and your Mexican pesos.

Élie Faure told me about your new Mexican love, but my feelings for you have not changed, and I have not looked for nor do I desire a new love. I sense that your Mexican love may be just a passing fancy for I

::

have reason to believe they often are. I know you do not write to Marievna either; you only send the money orders, no longer through me but through Adam Fischer, so as not to hurt me. As you can see, I am well informed, not because I try to find things out but because your friends and mine will tell me things all of a sudden, probably because they think they are doing me a favor by helping me wake up from the dream I live in. Élie Faure was very straightforward about it: "Angelina, you have always been a very sensible and well-balanced woman, you must build a new life for yourself. Everything with Diego has come to an end, and you are worth too much . . ." I no longer remember what else he said because I did not even listen, I did not want to believe him. When you left, Diego, I still had illusions. It seemed to me that in spite of everything, the strong bonds that united us remained firm, that they would never be definitively broken, that we could still be useful to one another. It is so painful for me to think that you do not need me any more, you who would always shout "Quiela" like a drowning man begging for someone to throw him a life raft.

Anyway, enough! I could continue writing indefinitely, but since you have so little time to waste perhaps this letter will seem too long. It is futile for me to ask you to write, nevertheless, you really should. You should especially answer this letter since it will be the last I will bother you with. Answer however you think best, but *en toutes lettres*. You need not give me many explanations, a few words would be enough, a telegram, the important thing is for you to tell me. I close with an affectionate hug,

Quiela

P.S. What do you think of my engravings?

P O S T S C R I P T

Bertram Wolfe, author of *The Fabulous Life of Diego Rivera*, supplied much of the information, including textual quotations, on which these letters are based. According to his book, Angelina Beloff, with the encouragement of her Mexican painter friends, traveled to the land of her dreams thirteen years later, in 1935. She did not look Diego up. She did not want to disturb him. When they met at a concert in a theater in Mexico City, Diego passed by without recognizing her.

ABOUT THE AUTHOR

Elena Poniatowska, born in Paris in 1933, is today one of Mexico's leading literary and intellectual figures. Novelist, essayist, and journalist, she was the first woman to win Mexico's prestigious National Journalism Award. Her major novel *Hasta no verte Jesús mío* will be published by Pantheon in 1987.